SeP2015

The Egyptian Cat Mystery

By Penny Dolan

Illustrated by Andy Elkerton

Crabtree Publishing Company

www.crabtreebooks.com

Crabtree Publishing Company
www.crabtreebooks.com
1-800-387-7650

616 Welland Ave.
St. Catharines, ON
L2M 5V6

PMB 59051, 350 Fifth Ave.
59th Floor,
New York, NY 10118

Published by Crabtree Publishing Company in 2016

First published in 2014 by Franklin Watts
(A division of Hachette Children's Books)

Text © Penny Dolan 2014
Illustration © Andy Elkerton 2014

Series editor: Melanie Palmer
Series advisor: Catherine Glavina
Series designer: Cathryn Gilbert
Editor: Kathy Middleton
**Proofreader and
  notes to adults:** Shannon Welbourn
**Production coordinator and
  Prepress technician:** Ken Wright
Print coordinator: Amy Salter

Printed in the USA/082015/SN20150529

**Library and Archives Canada
Cataloguing in Publication**

Dolan, Penny, author
    The Egyptian cat mystery / Penny Dolan ;
Andy Elkerton, illustrator.

(Race further with reading)
Issued in print and electronic formats.
ISBN 978-0-7787-2060-7 (bound).--
ISBN 978-0-7787-2108-6 (pbk.).--
ISBN 978-1-4271-1666-6 (pdf).--
ISBN 978-1-4271-1658-1 (html)

    I. Elkerton, Andy, illustrator II. Title.

PZ7.D665Eg 2015   j823'.92   C2015-903054-4
                                    C2015-903055-2

**Library of Congress
Cataloging-in-Publication Data**

CIP available at the Library of Congress

Chapter 1
The Egyptian Cat

"Hurry up!" cried Jed, running up the steps and into the museum. He and his big sister Ruby were speeding to their favorite spot: the Egyptian galleries. They liked to look at all the precious treasures and statues, and gaze at the mummies in their decorated cases.

Today, the galleries were almost empty. Jed and Ruby could look at the ancient wall paintings as long as they wanted.

"I'd like to be an Egyptian queen and sail along the Nile River," said Ruby, dreamily.

"Well, I'd like to ride in a chariot," Jed told her, "and feel the horses going really fast."

Then they spotted a poster. It read:

HAVE FUN ON A MUSEUM SLEEPOVER!

"I'd like to do that," Jed sighed.

"Me, too," said Ruby. But they both knew

it would cost too much.

After a while, Jed's stomach rumbled.

Ruby's did, too.

"Snack time," Ruby declared.

"I'm starving."

They sat down on a bench. Ruby opened up
her backpack.

"Yum, yum," she said.

"Ugh! Barbecued lobster potato chips?
Yuck!" grumbled Jed.

No
Eating

"She'd like them," Ruby joked, pointing
at the carved cat who sat proudly on a
pillar nearby.

"No way," Jed told Ruby. "That cat is too good for your fishy-smelling potato chips." Jed really admired the Egyptian cat. She had a narrow gold collar around her neck and tiny golden disks hanging from her ears.

"Sitting there forever must be so boring,"
Jed said. "Maybe there's a magical day
when she comes to life."

Ruby laughed. Just then the sun shone
through the windows and the cat's face
glowed. Jed was sure she had smiled at him.
Don't be silly, he thought to himself.

While they munched their apples, Ruby

told Jed a tale about an Egyptian princess.

Some said her ghost haunted the corridors

of the museum, although nobody knew why.

Jed liked the story, even if it wasn't true.

A worker wheeled a trolley toward them along the gallery. He scowled and glared hard at Ruby and Jed as if he wanted them to move.

"Should we go?" whispered Jed.

"No," said Ruby. "We're allowed to sit here. Oops! Well, maybe not eat here," she added nervously, spying a sign behind the bench.

No Eating

The man unloaded a big screen. He set it up all around the cat statue. He slapped a big "Keep Out" sticker on the outside, then went behind the screen himself.

"That's not fair," grumbled Jed.

"Now we can't see our cat."

Chapter 2
A Strange Event

As the clock struck three, the man behind the screen started chanting. He sang in an odd, high voice.

"That's a weird song. What's going on?" asked Jed.

"I don't know." Ruby frowned.

"Did you see that strange amulet hanging from the chain around his neck?"

Suddenly they heard shuffling and a sharp, cat-like cry. The man came out from behind the screen holding a big cardboard box and walked away quickly.

"That box looked just like a pet carrier," said Ruby. Jed peeked behind the screen. The beautiful Egyptian cat was gone!

EGYPTIAN CAT

"That man does work for the museum, doesn't he?" Jed wondered out loud.

"He must," said Ruby, uncertain.

Just then her phone beeped. "Anyway, it's time to go home, Jed. Mom says hurry up!"

They took the back staircase down to the gloomy corridor with the heavy, revolving doors. Jed was about to go through them when he stopped. A shadowy figure stared back at him through the dark glass. It wasn't his face. It wasn't Ruby's face either.

It was a ghostly woman. She wore a wide,
jeweled braid around her long, straight hair.
Her dark eyes, outlined with paint, looked
sad and angry. Who was Jed seeing? Ruby
was the only one behind him.

"It's the Egyptian princess!" he gasped.

"Stop messing around, Jed. Just go through the doors," Ruby grumbled.

"I can see her!" Jed cried.

"No way!" Ruby pushed Jed through the revolving doors. The figure immediately disappeared. But when the doors stopped spinning, Ruby stopped and stared. She gulped and pushed through the doors. Her eyes were wide. "I saw her, too! What does she want?"

Their bus was at the museum's stop, so Ruby grabbed Jed's hand. They rushed on board. "Stay next to me," she ordered. "Watch out for our stop."

The crowded bus inched through the traffic.

Suddenly Jed froze. Farther up the bus sat the strange man from the museum. He wore an ordinary coat. His eyes were closed, and he was holding the pet carrier.

"Ruby," Jed whispered. "Look! I'm sure he's got the cat!"

"We can't do anything," Ruby replied, as the bus squeezed under a railway bridge.

19

All at once, they saw a face appear next to them—the Egyptian princess! She seemed to be speaking, one silent word at a time: "Free—the—cat," she begged.

Immediately, they glanced at the cardboard box. It was bulging a bit. Then one edge split open and a black paw poked out.

"He's got a cat in there," Ruby whispered.

"Not any old cat," Jed told her. "It's the cat from the museum. Today's her magic day and he has cat-napped her."

It was all very well for the princess to ask them to save the cat, but how?

Chapter 3
Cat Rescue!

Their bus stop was coming up soon.

Ruby and Jed moved toward the door.

The man was fast asleep. Now they could

see two paws clawing away at the gap.

Jed thought about the ghostly princess.

"Free the cat!" That's what she had said.

So, carefully, Jed pushed one leg against the pet carrier. As he pushed, the hole gaped wider. Quickly, the cat slid out and smiled up at them. As the door of the bus opened, Ruby and Jed glanced at each other.

"Go!" Ruby whispered.

They shot out and away down the nearest street, on the heels of the cat. They saw the man wake up and struggle to his feet, but the doors had already closed. Too late! He was trapped inside the bus.

Jed and Ruby had saved the mysterious cat. "But what do we do with her now?" Ruby wondered.

The cat walked along between them,
proudly holding up her tail. The streetlights
shone on her golden collar and glinted off
the rings in her ears.

"What will we tell Mom?" Ruby said, as she
unlocked the front door.

"She'll be home soon."

Pets were not allowed in their apartment building, but that did not bother the cat. Meowing happily, she prowled around and made herself at home. She chose a corner in Jed's room just behind a chair and curled up into a ball. And not a moment too soon!

Mom came in, beaming.

"Did you have a good day at the museum?"

"Listen, kids, I've got to pop out for awhile after we eat dinner. Mrs. Brown from next door will look in on you. Is that okay?"

Ruby and Jed sighed happily.

"That's great, Mom," they said, relieved.

Once Mrs. Brown had turned on the TV, they could go and look after the magical black cat.

"She's so beautiful," said Ruby.

The cat woke up, gave a long, elegant stretch, and sprang up onto the windowsill. She nuzzled Jed's books about the Egyptians.

Suddenly she paused. She stared at the round, glass paperweight. Inside the glass sphere was a model of an ancient pyramid. All at once, the cat's eyes became two green full moons.

"Meow!" she cried, calling the children closer to her.

Chapter 4
Another World

Ruby and Jed saw the glass globe growing larger and larger, until it became an enormous shimmering bubble.

Suddenly they were inside the bubble—and in another place. It was hot, dry, and sunny. "It's ancient Egypt!" gasped Jed.

The air was scented with spices and desert dust. Sand crunched under their feet as the cat led them onward into a busy market full of people and animals.

Beyond the market were the banks of a vast river. The cat led them onto a sailing boat filled with dates and other fruit. The boat sailed up the river, passing between fields of grain. Jed and Ruby gazed around, but nobody stopped or stared at them at all.

After awhile, they reached a landing dock.
Jed and Ruby got off the boat, and the cat
led them toward a waiting chariot. They
held on tightly as the driver flicked the reins.
Off raced the horses along the wide road.

The chariot stopped at the entrance to a grand palace.

"Meow!" called the cat, taking Ruby and Jed into a great hall full of musicians and dancers. There, on a golden throne, sat a beautiful woman. She was smiling at them in a mysterious but friendly way.

"She's the only one who can see us," Jed said.

"The princess!" gasped Ruby.

Then, in front of them, they saw a necklace. The bird's wings were made from stones called turquoise. Its body and head were made of gold. One gleaming stone remained to be set into place. This is why the cat had brought them here. For some reason, the cat had chosen them to finish the necklace.

Ruby picked up the stone. The surface was carved with strange signs. As she placed the stone into Jed's palm, the gem glowed.

"It must be magical," Ruby said.

"It belongs in the necklace, doesn't it?" Jed said. "I think the cat wants us to make the necklace complete." As they put the stone in, the cat began to purr loudly.

Suddenly they were outside in the blazing sun of the courtyard. A blast of trumpets echoed around them. All the people lifted their heads and became as still and silent as statues or paintings.

The cat gave a strange cry. Everything shimmered and shone around them. The next thing they knew, the air smelled like home again. They were back in their own time. The cat was still with them, purring triumphantly.

Chapter 5
The Princess

"Ruby? Jed?" Mrs. Brown was calling them. "How are you kids doing? Your mom will be home in a moment." The cat had curled herself up behind the chair again.

"How can we get her back to the museum?" worried Ruby.

"I don't know," said Jed, looking uneasy.

Mom had only been home a moment when the doorbell rang.

"Who can that be?" Mom opened the door. They all stared. Outside in the dark was a tall, elegant woman with large painted eyes. She was wrapped in an ancient shawl, and her dark hair curled wildly around her head. She carried a large, battered straw basket under her arm.

"Good evening!" she began, in a voice that was as soft as a cat's purr.

"I'm Professor Akhten from the museum." Opening her basket, she held out two envelopes in her long, ring-covered fingers.

"Good news! Your children have won prizes in our "Young Egyptologists" contest."

The professor gave a dazzling smile.

"Our records show your children have visited the museum often." Mom nodded yes.

"Especially the Egyptian galleries."

Jed and Ruby nodded yes.

"We...we were there today," they stammered. Could this mysterious professor be who they thought she was? If only she would step into the light, they could see her better.

The professor smiled. "Yes, it was a day when we needed observant children around," she said mysteriously.

Ruby and Jed opened the envelopes.

"Sleepover tickets!" they cried.

"There's one for you, as well." The professor gave Mom a ticket, too.

Mom went pink with excitement.

"Oh, please come in," she said. "I'll just pop into the kitchen and put some coffee on."

The professor stayed in the shadows outside.

"I'm sorry. I can't come in," she explained.

"I have an important job to do."

She gave a curious low whistle.

"Meow!" Out from Jed's room ran the cat.

She twirled herself around the professor's

ankles, then leaped into the open basket,

purring happily.

"Sorry. It's later than I thought. I must go!" said the professor. Clutching the basket to her chest, the professor winked. "Well done, you two," she whispered. "The Egyptian cat is safe again. By placing the gem in the necklace you broke the curse that kept me as a ghost." Then she hurried off into the night.

"What a strange woman," Mom said.

"And what a wonderful princess," Jed whispered to Ruby.

The next morning, Mom double checked to make sure the sleepover tickets really were okay. Just as she was logging off from the museum website, she paused.

"Look at this!" There, on Mom's tablet, was the image of an ancient Egyptian princess. "It says here that she's supposed to haunt the museum. You know, she reminds me of somebody, but I can't think who."

Jed and Ruby just smiled.

the Museum

Notes for Adults

Race Further with Reading is the next entertaining level up for young readers from *Race Ahead with Reading*. Longer, more in-depth chapters and fun illustrations help children build up their vocabulary and reading skills in a fun way.

THE FOLLOWING BEFORE, DURING, AND AFTER READING ACTIVITY SUGGESTIONS SUPPORT LITERACY SKILL DEVELOPMENT AND CAN ENRICH SHARED READING EXPERIENCES:

BEFORE

1. Make reading fun! Choose a time to read when you and the reader are relaxed and have time to share the story together. Don't forget to give praise! Children learn best in a positive environment.
2. Before reading, ask the reader to look at the title and illustrations on the cover of the book **The Egyptian Cat Mystery**. Invite them to make predictions about what will happen in the story. They may make use of prior knowledge and make connections to other stories they have heard or read about a similar character.

DURING

3. Encourage readers to determine unfamiliar words themselves by using clues from the text and illustrations.
4. During reading, encourage the child to review his or her understanding and see if they want to revise their predictions midway. Encourage the reader to make text-to-text connections, choosing a part of the story that reminds them of another story they have read; and text-to-self connections, choosing a part of the story that relates to their own personal experiences; and text-to-world connections, choosing a part of the story that reminds them of something that happened in the real world.

AFTER

5. Ask the reader who the main characters are. Describe how the characters' traits or feelings impact the story.
6. Have the child retell the story in their own words. Ask him or her to think about the predictions they made before reading the story. How were they the same or different?

7. Encourage the reader to refer to parts in the story by the chapters the events occurred in and explain how the story developed.

DISCUSSION QUESTIONS FOR KIDS

8. Throughout this story, Jed and Ruby are faced with obstacles. What do they do to solve the problems and how do they react to the different events?
9. Choose one of the illustrations from the story. How do the details in the picture help you understand a part of the story better? Or, what do the illustrations tell you that is not in the text?
10. What part of the story surprised you? Why was it a surprise?
11. From your point of view, what did you think the image of the Egyptian princess would mean to Jed and Ruby?
12. What moral, or lesson, can you take from this story?
13. Create your own story or drawing about something you wish would come to life or a mystery that you solved.
14. Have you read another story by the same author? Compare the stories you have read by the same author or compare this story to other books in the *Race Further with Reading* series.
15. Have you ever had a sleepover? Describe what you think Jed and Ruby's experience will be like when they sleepover at the museum.